To: Denese,
my dear
Grand aughter.
Love, G. Foye , 1996

Ride the Red Cycle

Ride the

Illustrated by David Brown

To my husband, McLouis Robinet,
who builds cycles and fulfills dreams

Ride the Red Cycle

"Jerome's got something to say, Mama, and you gotta listen!"

Jerome felt a warm blush rise up from his neck as Tilly, his fifteen-year-old sister, spoke for him. He wished she wouldn't do that. It made him feel he wasn't real.

Once he had liked the word *special,* special classes, special bus. Then he decided it meant "not like other boys."

The trouble was that people were always helping him. His speech was slow and slurred, and someone was always finishing what he wanted to say. When he played baseball, he would kneel to bat the ball and someone would run the bases for him. When he tried to roll his wheelchair at school, one of the kids would insist on pushing it. Everything happened to him, but he never got a chance to make things happen himself. Like a chick breaking out of an egg, he wanted to break free.

Sitting at the breakfast table on that sunny spring morning, he felt a little dizzy; his heart beat faster, the room looked fuzzy to him. It was now or never, he thought. Would they laugh at him? It didn't matter, this was something he had to do. He had to make a break, and this was how he was going to do it. There was a dream that haunted him, and he had to do something about that dream. He wished he spoke more clearly, but since he couldn't, he asked very slowly.

"I wann tricycle to rrr-ride!"

"How's Jerome gonna ride, when he can't walk yet, Papa?" Liza asked innocently. Jerome picked up his fork and struck her on the arm; when she screamed, he made a face at her.

"Jerome, you stop that!" Mama said. She looked thin and nervous, her fingers tapped on the table.

Round-faced Liza was only five, but already she could ride Tilly's big two-wheeler. She didn't mean to hurt anyone when she reminded the family that eleven-year-old Jerome, who was in the fifth grade, couldn't even walk.

As a baby, he had walked at nine months. By his first birthday he was running around strong. But when he was two years old, a virus infection had gone to his brain and left damage that affected his whole body. When he got better, he had to learn to support his head, turn over, and crawl all over again. And his legs remained crippled.

Nervous and angry, Mama began clearing the breakfast table even though no one was finished. Papa, Liza, Tilly, and plump little three-year-old Gordon grabbed at toast as Mama whisked plates away.

"That ungrateful boy," Mama grumbled, "never says thank you, but always demandin' somethin'. It's take him here, take him there. Clinics, doctors, physical therapy, speech therapy. Seems that's all I do, take Jerome Johnson somewheres. Now he want a tricycle at eleven years old. Lordy, what's comin' next?"

Papa, a short stocky man with dark brown skin, cleared his throat. "What *they* say, Mary?"

Jerome felt angry tears springing into his eyes. He felt so angry he hit Gordon under the table and Gordon started to cry. Jerome's throat ached from wanting to cry, too, but he couldn't blink or someone would notice.

He didn't mind what Mama said, she was always grumbling. Besides, Mama was fussing because she was scared that her big son couldn't ride a tricycle. He knew how his mother felt because he was scared himself. But

how would he ever find out if he never tried? No, he wasn't angry with Mama, but Papa wanted to know what *they* had to say.

All his life *they*—all the people in his life that other boys never had to worry about—got to say things about him.

They were the physical therapists who exercised his legs, the speech therapists, the bone doctors, the nerve doctors, the eye doctors, and the social workers who got money for Mama to pay for his braces and his special shoes and his eyeglasses and his wheelchair. *They* were all the people he had to be grateful to. He was tired of being grateful. He hated to say thank you, it got stuck in his throat.

They made all the decisions in his life; but just once he wanted to do something all by himself! This time he didn't care what *they* said. He had thought for a long time, and he had chosen carefully for himself. A teen-ager with cerebral palsy told him that a two-wheeler was out of the question, it took balance to ride a two-wheeler. But three wheels . . .

Of course he was pleased with the wheelchair. He got around the neighborhood with it, except for curbs. Un-

6

til he was six, his folks had carried him like a bundle of newspapers.

The wheelchair was all right, but Jerome had a wonderful dream. In it he was speeding fast, with the wind in his face, eyes squinted tight, leaning forward like the leather-jacket guys on motorcycles. That was his dream, and in his dream hundreds of thousands watched as he

raced along a track. Cheers and clapping sounded like thunder in the sky. He was reckless and calm and cool, and millions knew his name. And as he stepped off his cycle, he walked with a casual swagger. Jerome Johnson, cycle rider!

All right, he couldn't race a motorcycle, but he had seen a gray-haired man on a three-wheel cycle once, the kind of cycle he wanted. Summer vacation started in a few weeks, and with real wheels he would be able to go everywhere. He didn't care what *they* said. Oh! for a set of wheels!

*

Mama answered Papa softly.

"John, physical therapist say it be good leg motion, good for his legs. But Dr. Ryan say that left leg real spastic-stiff."

Then in a louder voice aimed at Jerome, she said, " 'Sides, that boy's gotta learn to be grateful for what he got!"

"Ha!" Papa jumped at the mention of Dr. Ryan. "Dr. Ryan didn't think he could learn to crawl neither, but he did. I think the boy oughta have a tricycle!"

"Hey now, Papa!" Tilly said triumphantly. "Jerome

and me'll be ready to go shopping when you come home."
Saturdays Papa worked half-day at the post office.

Mama finished clearing the breakfast table and went
to tell the news to Mrs. Mullarkey, the next-door neigh-
bor. Liza, her round face grinning, and little brother
Gordon ran out to play. Tilly, tall and thin, dug her
hands into her skirt pockets and followed. She sighed. It
looked like Jerome was off again. But she knew that no
matter what he did, she'd always back him up.

Jerome sat alone in his wheelchair. He wore a green
shirt and short brown pants that he hated because his
leg braces showed. He was so excited that his eyeglasses
steamed up on the inside. He took them off and cleaned
them with a tissue. When he put them back on, the room
changed from a lazy blur to the sharply outlined kitchen.
The round table and chairs showed a hint of white paint
on their scrubbed wooden surfaces. Dishes were stacked
neatly on clean open shelves across from him.

He had worn eyeglasses since the virus. He thought
they made him look smart, like a professor; other people
said he looked like an angry owl. These particular glasses
were a victory for him. When he broke his last frames, he
had demanded thick black rims.

"I won't wear any pale eyeglasses," he had said.

But the eyeglass man said, "We don't have black rims for a child that age . . ."

While the man was talking, Tilly found some in the eyeglass catalogue. It took an extra two weeks for them to come, but at last he got the thick black frames for his big, sparkling black eyes.

He had to admit Tilly sometimes knew how he felt. She was the one who made sure the kids called him his full name. He hated being called Jerry; it sounded like a girl's name or a baby's name to him. With Tilly's help he was called Jerome. He thought Jerome Johnson had a noble sound!

And he liked his extra-strong brown arms and broad shoulders too. His arms had grown strong from support-ing him when his legs wouldn't. But he hated his skinny legs and the braces he wore attached to high-top shoes. None of that would matter, though, when he got his three-wheel cycle.

Whirling in his chair, he saw a limp balloon on the kitchen sideboard. It was one Gordon had been playing with. He reached over, grabbed it and tried to pop it with his broad clumsy hands. Straining violently, half-

afraid but wanting to hear the loud bang, he grunted, "Brrr-reak balloonnn."

It was too hard. His hands were too stiff to pop the silly old balloon. Something else he couldn't do.

Outside, Gordon overheard Jerome say "break balloon" just as Papa was coming home from work. Breathless, Gordon met his father.

"Papa, papa," Gordon called. "Jerome's gonna make the moon—he gonna ride his cycle to the moon, Papa?"

Papa smiled wearily and hugged Gordon. He didn't know where that little boy got his wild ideas! Inside, Tilly and Jerome were ready to go shopping, and they were soon on their way.

In the bicycle shop window, Jerome saw what he wanted. The seat was higher than those on small two-wheelers, the wheels were really big, and the color was orange-fire red. It was redder than any fire engine would dare to be.

"Papa, Uh wannn-n tha' un," he called out.

Oh! He could feel the wind whizzing through his soft black kinky hair as he sped along the highways. Highways? Well, along the sidewalk anyway.

Tilly pushed his wheelchair straight up to the big three-

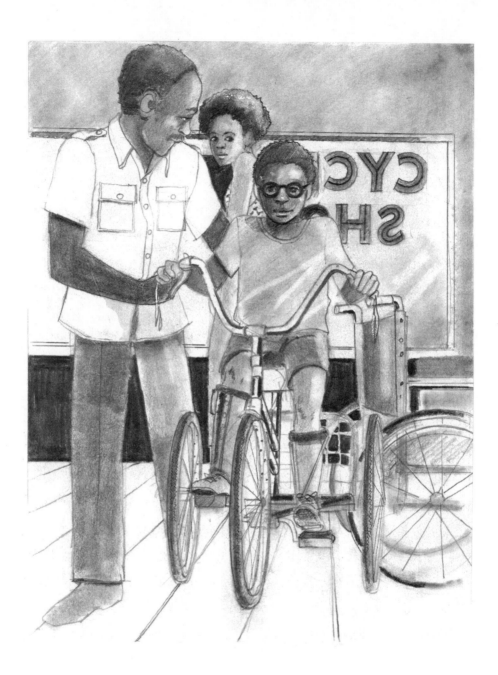

wheel cycle while Papa went to get a salesman. There was no price tag on the cycle, and he was afraid to hope. His heart beat faster and he felt breathless for the second time that day. He was so close, this was the cycle he wanted. Would it cost too much?

He was thrilled and happy and afraid too. Maybe Mama was right and he was being foolish. Just then Jerome saw Tilly's foot. He turned his wheelchair quickly and ran over it. He didn't mean to exactly, but he was anxious and getting angry. Papa hadn't come back yet.

Tilly yelled out and looked at him sharply. Why was her brother so mean? Here she was backing him up and he was mean to her again. Why did she ever bother with Jerome? The hurt brought tears to her eyes, but Jerome didn't say he was sorry.

Papa came back and lifted his son onto the seat of the big red cycle. It must be all right; he'll buy it for me, Jerome thought. He gripped the handles and noticed red and white streamers on the plastic handle grips—how they would fly in the wind as he rode! But he felt shaky, up so high on the seat, and as he held on and looked around, Papa noticed.

"Never you mind, son, I'll build up the pedals and make

the seat broader," Papa told him. Then to the salesman he said, "We'll take this 'un."

Papa paid at the cash register, and soon Jerome was riding home with his dream cycle tied down in the trunk of the car.

At the house, Mama and Mrs. Mullarkey were standing in the sunshine talking. Jerome was glad Mama hadn't gone to the bicycle shop. She would have made a fuss over the price and would have made him thank Papa, thank the salesman. He didn't thank anybody.

"Lord-a-mighty! What's that?" Mama said, shocked at the big, bright-red, shiny cycle.

"Boy's gonna kill himself on that, Mary!" Mrs. Mullarkey whispered.

Jerome slid out of the car onto the sidewalk. He crawled past Tilly who reached to help him; he crawled past Papa who unfolded his wheelchair for him. He kneeled up straight and, looking at Mama and Mrs. Mullarkey, he said slowly, "Here muhhh cycle. Papa gonna fit it for to rrr-ride!"

Then he lumbered across the grass, up the steps, and into the house. He would show them, maybe, he thought. Everyone watched him in silence.

Suddenly Mama called after him. "Hope yuh told yuh Papa thank you!"

Papa frowned at Mama and said, "Boy don't havta be beholdin' to no one."

Tilly thought, he could've said he was sorry, though, when he ran over my foot.

It took Papa almost a week of evenings after work to

finish outfitting the cycle. He attached wooden blocks to the pedals and put leather straps on the blocks to hold his son's shoes. Without the straps Jerome couldn't keep his feet on the pedals.

Since his son kept sliding off the seat, Papa made a new one. From a secondhand chair he got a plastic seat and back, all in one piece. He drilled holes and screwed the new seat onto the cycle, then put a seat belt around it.

On the first of June, Jerome sat on his cycle outdoors for the first time, but he didn't try riding until Papa came home. Everyone was excited. Kids and their mothers from the other row houses on the block gathered on his front doorsteps. For the millionth time Mama told them how much trouble he had been because he wasn't grateful for just being alive.

"Lordy, I never thought my boy'd be livin' today, the way he was. He lay there two weeks, didn't know nobody. All but dead before he come to." Mama was always harping on how sick he had been with the virus.

One mother told Mama he was a brave boy, but Mama shook her head. "Stubborn and foolish," she said.

Neighborhood kids were riding their bicycles in circles and then standing astride them. Liza, a proud grin across her face, rode up and down the block calling people to come see her brother's new cycle.

Jerome thought Mama looked a little proud of him in spite of what she said. She stood on the steps with her thin arms crossed tightly. He was glad people were calling it a cycle and not a tricycle. It was big enough not to look like the tricycles little Gordon's friends rode.

When Papa came home, he pulled his son's handlebars slowly and showed him how to push from his knees to pedal. Jerome leaned forward panting, his tongue showing, but his legs wouldn't move. His legs wouldn't move!

He wiped at the silver stream of drool that soaked his shirt. He only drooled now when he was nervous, and with all those people watching, he was nervous. His legs trembled and he felt cold with his sweat and saliva drying in the breeze.

After a while the neighbors and kids grew tired of watching him and they agreed it would be a long time before he learned to ride, if ever. As they began drifting away, he felt disappointment drape over him like a dead man's shirt. He didn't really expect to ride the first day, but somehow he had hoped . . .

The kids went their ways, calling noisily to each other

and racing off on bicycles, but Papa and Tilly stayed, giving him pushes.

"Papa, yook, eh catch," Jerome whispered to his father. At each rotation of the wheel, the brace on his left leg caught in the front wheel. Papa shifted his foot further.

"I'll put a shield on the sides to keep them braces from catchin'," he told his son.

The shields did keep the braces from catching in the wheel, but they didn't make Jerome's legs turn the wheels of the cycle. He spent every afternoon after school sitting and trying to rock his cycle, but he never moved. Sometimes kids came along and pulled or pushed him.

He had been able to get around by himself in the wheelchair, but now he often got stranded on his cycle. The kids would go in and leave him around the corner or down the street and he couldn't follow them. When dinner time came, Mama or Tilly had to go looking for him. Mama now added *contrary* to *ungrateful* when she fussed at him.

And then something exciting happened. One day he was turning the handlebars, weaving back and forth, as some boys ran behind pushing him. One sharp turn and the red cycle fell over. Mama fussed about the bump on his forehead and his scraped knee, but he felt happy and victorious.

"Yook, Papa," he called later when Papa came in from work. "Uh gohh Band-Aid. Uh busted muh knee."

He had calluses on his knees and hands from crawling, but he never had a good hurt knee before. Now he had joined all those other kids who got to wear Band-Aids on their knees. Somehow it made him feel he was really learning to ride. Other kids fell off bicycles when they were learning to ride, and he had fallen too. That night he thought and thought and came up with a plan.

"Eh, Tilly," he called the next day. "Take muh up by alley where slants to da strrrr-eet."

"Trucks come in the alley by the factory, Jerome. You gotta stay on the sidewalk," Tilly told him.

"Buttt Tilly, yuh be wid muh," he begged. "I cann-nn rrr-ride dere."

So Tilly pulled him along the block, not telling anyone where they were going. When they reached the alley, she sat in the uncut grass and chickweed watching for cars and reading a book. She enjoyed the peace and quiet. No one was around, so Jerome could grunt and sway all he needed, trying to pedal.

Three weeks passed and school was out. Every morning Tilly and Jerome went on their secret trip for a couple of hours. When Mama asked them where they went all morning, Jerome said, "Uh beennn near."

Mama accepted the fact that he stayed close, but Gordon could hardly wait to tell Papa that evening.

"Papa, Jerome say he drink beer and Mama didn't tell him nothing!"

Soon Jerome could shake the cycle enough on the slope so that his right leg got down fast enough for the left leg to reach the top of its pedal. Then he could grunt the stiff left leg down. He pedaled, but not always. He never could be sure. The dream of success was becoming a nightmare. He felt foolish and silly, not being able to depend on his rotten old legs.

"Tilly donnn' tellll," he begged. Every day they went to the alley. Tilly pulled the cycle out of the way when trucks came up to the factory, then she put her brother back on the slope and sat yawning, chin in hands, watching him struggle with the red cycle. What was simple for a three-year-old was hard for her eleven-year-old brother!

Sometimes she wished he were somebody else's brother; sometimes she almost hated him, he was so stubborn and

mean. Her head got all confused when Jerome was mean, and she often felt she didn't love him at all, but she stuck by him all the time.

By July he could ride down the slant, but he fought and struggled to ride up. Soon his legs moved one after the other, and he was riding. Some days Jerome nearly burst with triumph and Tilly wanted to tell Mama and Papa right away. But other days there was only failure. On those days his legs wouldn't push as he wished; in fact, they wouldn't move at all. He had nightmares about his legs not working when he tried to show Mama. In his dreams, Mama and Papa were watching and his legs wouldn't budge. His legs must learn to move one after the other all the time. He knew it wouldn't be easy and he was fighting hard. Gradually he became more sure of being able to pedal; his legs worked more often than they didn't.

In August smothering heat arrived, but Jerome forced his legs to move in spite of the sweat pouring off him. Besides Tilly, no one else knew how hard he was trying.

At home Mama was afraid to hope; it broke her heart to watch him sit still out front on that red cycle. Papa was afraid not to hope.

By then the kids on the block had decided that Jerome would never ride. He had been fun the way he was; if only he would be satisfied with himself. What was so important about riding that cycle?

The summer before, he had played baseball with the other kids and Tommy usually ran bases for him. But this summer he tripped Tommy and made his nose bleed. Then David ran his bases one day and Jerome threw a stone at him and David needed an ice pack. Now all Jerome did was sit alone on the big red cycle. The kids thought he was mean and they stopped playing with him. Why did he want that big cycle anyway?

But Jerome had his dream and he had chosen it carefully. It was something he could do, it was possible, and he would do it. It was one thing he would get to do all by himself. Tilly, it was true, brought him to the slanted drive, but *he* was the one fighting his legs to ride. He'd show Tommy and David and all the kids—he'd even show Tilly, because there was something secret he was practicing late at night all by himself.

*

By the end of August he could hardly wait to show off. As he became sure of himself, the perfect occasion came up. The neighbors planned a block party for Labor Day weekend.

That Saturday morning police closed the street at both ends, and teen-agers decorated trees with yellow crepe-paper banners. Neighbors held brightly colored balloons, and marching music filled the air. Everyone was dressed in cool, colorful clothes for the hot summer day.

In the morning there was a pet parade, then games with water-filled balloons. Artists of all ages drew pictures on the sidewalk with colored chalk. In the afternoon there was a program of local talent.

David played drums, Liza sang a funny song, and another girl arranged a mushroom dance with five little girls. Jerome knew that Tilly had put his name next on the program.

For the mushroom dance the little girls held umbrellas covered with brown paper. Everyone liked the silly twirling dance, and when they finished, Mrs. Mullarkey called out, "And next on our program is Jerome Johnson who will, who will . . . Jerome Johnson, folks!"

Everyone clapped politely. Then there was an eerie quiet. Adults and kids looked at one another to see if anyone knew what was going to happen. What was he going to do?

Tilly pulled her brother out into the street at the end of the block, and left him sitting on the shiny orange red cycle. Her heart was pounding and she lowered her head and stuck her hands in her jean pockets as she strolled away from him. He was on his own.

Mama folded her arms to calm herself; Papa sat down on the curb because his knees grew weak. Liza hugged Gordon and waited. Gordon wondered if his brother would go to the moon now.

Jerome, frowning and gritting his teeth, struggled for what seemed like hours to get his legs moving. After two long minutes, slowly but firmly, he began pedaling—gripping the handles and leaning forward as though he were speeding along. There was no wind whipping in his face, but that didn't matter. He was riding his cycle himself; he was riding. That was all he could think.

The neighbors murmured and nodded to each other. Mrs. Mullarkey forgot she was holding the loudspeaker and blew her nose. The noise made everyone giggle nervously.

His progress down the street was slow, deliberate, and strangely rhythmic. People could hardly wait to applaud and, as he neared the end, clapping burst forth and the kids cheered, but he remained calm and cool.

"O.K.," he muttered to himself, "wid Tilly's help Uh learnnnn tuh ride. But nnnnnn-now Uh really show um."

He stopped in the middle of the street, opened the seat belt, and bowed with a flourish to the people on his right. When he bowed, he made sure he slipped his right foot out of the pedal strap. He bowed and waved to the people clapping on his left and slipped his left foot out of the pedal strap just as he had planned. His hands trembled.

Tilly wondered why he had stopped in the middle. She started toward him, but he stopped her with an icy scowl. Papa stood up, but Jerome frowned at him too.

Mama muttered, "Lordy, ain't enough he can ride, that silly boy gonna crawl off in the middle of the street."

The neighbors got quiet again.

Carefully Jerome slid his right leg around and off the cycle. He stood crouched on both feet, his knees and hips bent under his weight. He was grateful for the braces that kept his feet flat on the ground. At night when he had practiced this with his braces off, he stood on his toes.

He heard himself saying, "Uh wannn-na tank evv-body help muh, 'pecially muh sister Tilly, and muh Papa, and muh Mama." He nodded at Mama—he had said thank you and it didn't stick in his throat this time. There was a mild sprinkling of applause.

Then, while eighty people held their breath, he let go of the cycle. His arms wavered at his sides, balancing him. His head was high, his chin jutted forward. In spite of his eyeglasses everybody and everything was blurred.

He slid his stiff left leg forward, feet and knees twisted in; then he stepped jerkily off on his right foot. He dragged his left leg, stepped with his right. Deliberate, slow, arms waving in the air, one leg after the other, Jerome Johnson walked. It was stiff and clumsy walking, with twisted legs, but these were his first steps, practiced late at night.

Before he reached his wheelchair, he fell to the street. No one moved toward him. Clapping and cheering could be heard for five blocks. It was almost like thunder in the sky. His dream had come true.

He didn't try to get to his feet again, he crawled to his wheelchair. He'd work on walking with his physical therapist now that it wasn't a secret anymore. Now that he'd shown them how much he could do all by himself.

Mama was thanking the Lord, Papa cried and didn't care who saw him. Liza and Gordon were staring with mouths hanging open. For Gordon, his brother's going to the moon had seemed a simple thing; his brother's walking was far more wonderful.

Tilly rolled on the grass, laughing and crying and hugging herself for joy. Her tough, stubborn little brother had learned to ride a cycle and had taught himself to walk.

Jerome saw Tommy and David among the neighbors. Maybe he'd play some baseball with them. After all, he could walk now. Maybe next summer he would be running—even running his own bases.

Maybe he'd even . . .

Jerome was dreaming again.